SQUIRREL NUTKIN

Based on the original story by
Beatrix Potter
with all new illustrations

Cover illustration by
Anita Nelson
Book illustrations by
Pat Schoonover

Publications International, Ltd.

They made little rafts out of twigs, and they paddled over the water to Owl Island to gather nuts. Each squirrel had a little sack and a little oar; they spread their tails for sails.

They also took with them three fat mice as a present for Old Brown. The squirrels put the mice on his front doorstep. Twinkleberry and the other little squirrels bowed and said politely, "Old Mr. Brown, may we please have permission to gather nuts on your island?"

But Nutkin's manners were very rude. He bounced up and down like a little red cherry, singing—

> "Riddle me, riddle me,
>   rot-tot-tote!
> A little wee man,
>   in a red red coat!
> A staff in his hand,
>   and a stone in his throat;
> If you tell me this riddle,
>   I'll give you a groat."

Now, Mr. Brown was not at all interested in a groat, which is a coin. He went to sleep. The squirrels filled their sacks with nuts and sailed home in the evening.

The next morning the squirrels returned with a fat mole for Old Brown. But Nutkin began to tickle the sleeping Mr. Brown with a twig. Mr. Brown woke up and carried the mole into his house. He shut the door in Nutkin's face. Soon a little thread of blue smoke came up from the top of the tree. Nutkin peeked through the keyhole and sang—

"A house full, a hole full!
And you cannot gather a bowl full!"

The squirrels gathered nuts. But Nutkin watched Old Brown's door.

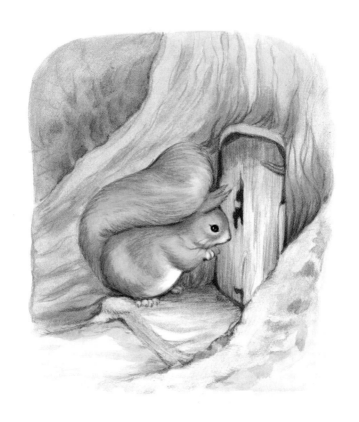

On the third day the squirrels went fishing. They caught seven fat minnows for Old Brown and paddled to Owl Island. Seven squirrels each carried a minnow. But Nutkin, who did not have nice manners, brought no present at all. He ran in front, singing.

Mr. Brown was not interested in songs. The squirrels filled their sacks with nuts. But Nutkin played a bowling game with pinecones.

On the fourth day the squirrels went to Owl Island for the last time. They brought an egg as a good-bye present for Old Brown. But Nutkin ran in front laughing and shouting—

"Humpty Dumpty lies in the beck,
With a white counterpane
   round his neck,
Forty doctors and forty wrights,
Cannot put Humpty Dumpty
   to rights!"

Now Mr. Brown liked eggs. He opened one eye and shut it again. But he still did not speak.

Then Nutkin became very rude—
"Old Mr. B! Old Mr. B!

> Hickamore, Hackamore,
>   on the King's kitchen door;
> All the King's horses,
>   and all the King's men,
> Couldn't drive Hickamore,
>   Hackamore,
> Off the King's kitchen door."

Nutkin danced about like a sunbeam. But still Old Brown said nothing at all.

Nutkin took a running jump right onto the head of Old Brown! All at once there was a fluttering and a scuffling and a loud "Squeak!" The other squirrels scampered away into the bushes. And when they came back very cautiously, peeking around the tree, there was Old Brown sitting on his doorstep. He sat quite still, with his eyes closed, as if nothing had happened.

But Nutkin was in his coat pocket!

This looks like the end of the story, but it isn't. Old Brown carried Nutkin into his house, and held him up by the tail, intending to eat him. But Nutkin struggled so very hard that his tail broke in two. He dashed up the stairs and escaped out of the attic window!

And to this day, if you meet Squirrel Nutkin and ask him a riddle, he will throw sticks at you, stamp his feet, scold, and shout, "Cuck-cuck-cuck-cur-r-r-cuck-k-k!"